Candletown
Can you find Puddle Lane?

USING THIS BOOK

*One of the best ways of helping children learn to read is to read stories to them and with them. This way they learn what **reading** is, and they will gradually come to recognize many words and begin to read for themselves.*

First, read the story on the left-hand pages aloud to the child.

Reread the story as often as the child enjoys hearing it. Talk about the pictures as you go.

Later the child will be able to read the words under the pictures on the right-hand pages.

Note: Small animals sometimes die because they go into discarded glass bottles and cannot get out again. An opportunity to explain this to children occurs in this story.

LADYBIRD BOOKS, INC.
Lewiston, Maine 04240 U.S.A.
© Text and layout SHEILA McCULLAGH MCMLXXXVI
© In publication LADYBIRD BOOKS LTD MCMLXXXVI
Loughborough, Leicestershire, England

Printed in England

Tom Cat and the Wideawake Mice

written by SHEILA McCULLAGH
illustrated by PRUE THEOBALDS

This book belongs to:

Ladybird Books

If you have not yet read Book 6, Stage 1,
***The Wideawake Mice**, read this aloud first.*

The Wideawake Mice were toy mice
in Mr. Wideawake's toy store.
One evening, the Magician
came into the store.
He didn't see the Wideawake Mice,
but he accidentally spilled some magic dust
all over them.
When the moon shone on them
later that night,
the Wideawake Mice came to life.
They crept out of the shop
through a hole under the door, and
found themselves in the street.

This story tells what happened next.

the Wideawake Mice

The Wideawake Mice looked
up and down the street.
The moon was shining down.
The houses towered up into the sky.
The Wideawake Mice felt very frightened.
They had never been outside
in the street before.

The Wideawake Mice
looked up and
down the street.

"I don't like it," said Uncle Maximus.
"I don't like it at all.
Let's go back into the store."

"Nonsense!" said Grandfather Mouse.
"We're going to find a home of our own."
Uncle Maximus looked very doubtful.

"You can't go back," said Aunt Jane.
"You'll never get back through the hole."

"You can't go back,"
said Aunt Jane.

"This way!" said Grandfather Mouse.
He set off down the street.
The other mice followed him.
At the end of the street,
they came to the square.
It looked very big and very wide.

"Where should we go now?"
asked Aunt Matilda.
"There's nowhere **to** go, that I can see,"
said Uncle Maximus.

"This way," said
Grandfather Mouse.

"What's over there?" asked Miranda,
looking across the square.

There was a market building
in the middle of the square.

"There might be a hole under it,"
said Jeremy.
"This way," said Grandmother Mouse.
"We'll go and see."

"This way," said
Grandmother Mouse.

Tom Cat was lying curled up
in a doorway.
He was fast asleep.

As the mice went out
into the square,
Tom Cat opened one eye.
He saw the Wideawake Mice.

Tom Cat
opened one eye.

Tom Cat woke up.
He was suddenly wide awake.
He was so surprised, that,
for a few moments,
he didn't move.
He had often seen mice before.
(He sometimes ate one for breakfast.)
But he had never seen mice
like the Wideawake Mice
in his life, until now.

Tom Cat woke up.

Very softly, Tom Cat got up.
Very slowly, he moved out,
into the moonlight.
Aunt Jane stopped.
She hadn't seen the cat, and
she hadn't heard the cat.
But she felt that there was
someone watching her.

Tom Cat got up.

Aunt Jane looked around.
She saw Tom Cat!

"Run!" cried Aunt Jane.
"Run for your lives!"

The little mice ran
as fast as they could.
They ran across the square
in the moonlight.

Aunt Jane
saw Tom Cat.

Tom Cat bounded out
into the square.
He ran after the Wideawake Mice.

Tom Cat ran after
the Wideawake Mice.

The Wideawake Mice ran away.
They ran as fast as they could.
But they didn't know how to run.
They ran along on their two back feet.

"Oh dear! Oh dear!"
cried Aunt Matilda.
"What can we do?
What **can** we do?"

Uncle Maximus was running so hard
that he didn't have enough breath left
to answer her.

The Wideawake Mice
ran away.

When they came to the market building,
Tom Cat was close behind them.

There was no time to climb a wall.

An empty bottle lay on the ground,
just outside the building.

Aunt Jane saw the bottle.
"Look!" she cried.
"We can hide in there."

Aunt Jane
saw the bottle.

One after another, the Wideawake Mice
went into the bottle.
They slithered through the narrow
glass neck, and slid right down into it.
Miranda and Jeremy went first.
Grandmother Mouse went next.
Aunt Matilda tumbled after her.
Uncle Maximus nearly got stuck,
but Aunt Jane gave him a big push.

Miranda and Jeremy
went into the bottle.

Grandfather followed Uncle Maximus,
and Aunt Jane went last.
She scrambled into the neck of the bottle.
Her tail was still hanging out,
when Tom Cat arrived.
Tom Cat jumped.
He made a grab for her tail,
but Aunt Jane pulled it
into the bottle just in time.

Tom Cat jumped.

Tom Cat stood and looked at the bottle.
He put a paw on it, and
rolled the bottle over.
All the little mice fell higgledy-piggledy,
one on top of the other.

Tom Cat looked at
the bottle.

Just then,
there was a loud "WOOF!"
The big dog who lived
at the end of Puddle Lane
had seen Tom Cat in the moonlight.
He came bounding across the square.
Tom Cat took one look at the dog,
and fled.
Tom Cat and the dog disappeared
behind the market building.

The dog saw Tom Cat.

"Oh dear!" said Aunt Matilda.

"I wish we had never left the store."

"Don't you wish any such thing,"
said Grandmother Mouse, sitting up.

"We're going to find a home for ourselves.
We'd better climb out of this bottle
while we can."

The glass was very slippery,
but Grandfather Mouse took off his coat,
and spread it on the glass,
and they all climbed over it.

They all got out of the bottle safely.

The Wideawake Mice
got out of the bottle.

"Where should we go now?"
puffed Uncle Maximus.
"Let's climb this post," said Aunt Jane.
"We might find a shelf at the top."
"I can't climb that,"
said Uncle Maximus.
"You can if you take off your shoes,"
said Aunt Jane.
The Wideawake Mice
all took off their shoes.
They ran up the post
to the roof of the market building.

The Wideawake Mice
ran up a post.

They found a dark shelf
under the roof.
"This is just the place for us,"
said Grandmother Mouse.
The mice were so tired
after all their adventures,
that they settled down quickly
in the shadows under the roof.
In a very few minutes,
they were fast asleep.
They were safe in their new home.

The Wideawake Mice
were fast asleep.

Can you remember
the names of the
Wideawake Mice?

Miranda Mouse

Aunt Jane

Jeremy Mouse

42

Aunt Matilda

Uncle Maximus

Grandmother Mouse

Grandfather Mouse

43

Notes for the parent/teacher

Turn back to the beginning and print the child's name in the space on the title page, using ordinary, not capital letters.

Now go through the book again. Look at each picture and talk about it. Point to the caption and read it aloud yourself.

Run your finger under the words as you read, so that the child learns that reading goes from left to right.

Encourage the child to read the words under the illustrations. Don't rush in with the word before he/she has had time to think, but don't leave him/her struggling.

Read this story as often as the child likes hearing it. The more opportunities he/she has to look at the illustrations and **read** the captions with you, the more he/she will come to recognize the words.

If you have several books, let the child choose which story he/she would like.

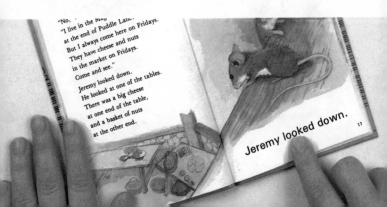

"No.
"I live in the Mill
at the end of Puddle Lane.
But I always come here on Fridays.
They have cheese and nuts
in the market on Fridays.
Come and see."
Jeremy looked down.
He looked at one of the tables.
There was a big cheese
at one end of the table,
and a basket of nuts
at the other end.

Jeremy looked down.

17